T0114587
9030 00007 0429 4

For my son Sorley

& my parents Sarah and Alexander

FLORA McDONNELL

Out of a Dark Winter's Night

Out of a dark winter's night…

comes light

and a spirit of adventure.

But day has to end

and give way
to night.

Surely something
can be done
to put this right?

With equipment,
friends,

and a hunch.

In spite of the weather

and how tiring
it turns out to be

losing lots of things on the way

not knowing

but never giving up.

Even if it means
getting into deep water

without being able to swim

and it feels like there is nothing
and nobody forever.

But then…

when no more can be done

hope comes to carry you…

home.

Thank you, Susanna
Queen of Elephants

First published in the United Kingdom in 2020 by Thames & Hudson Ltd,
181A High Holborn, London WC1V 7QX

British Library Cataloguing-in-Publication Data
A catalogue record for this book is available from the British Library

ISBN 978-0-500-65195-7

Printed and bound in China by Shanghai Offset Printing Products Limited